Bibble and the Bubbles

by Alice Hemming

Illustrated by Sara Sanchez

For Clara & Tommy

Bobby liked blowing bubbles.

Loopy bubbles, gloopy bubbles,
even stretchy, droopy bubbles.

Some went **pop** on next door's hedge,
some went sailing over the roof,
and some just floated up, **up**, **up**.

Where did they go?

667 million miles away stood Bibble.

Bibble liked catching bubbles.

LOOPY bubbles, gloopy bubbles, even stretchy, droopy bubbles. He had quite a collection.

Some bubbles **bounced** from crater to crater, some **drifted** between the stars and some just appeared.

Where did they come from?

One day, the bubbles stopped.
Bibble waited and waited but
they didn't come.

He had to find out why.

He took his collection of bubbles and worked away,

putting a **springy** bubble here and a **bouncy** bubble there,

until he had built...

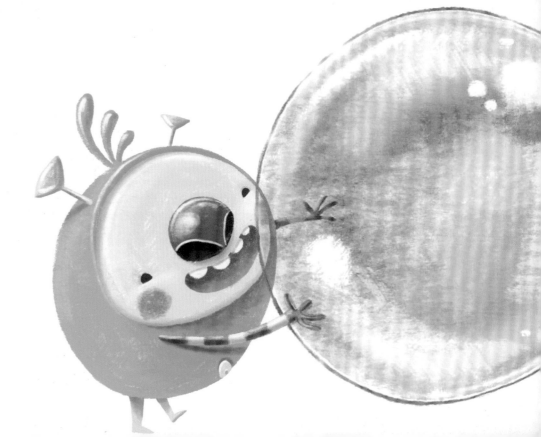

...a spaceship!

Bibble got
inside, pressed
a bubble button and
in a second he was off!

667 million miles away, Bobby's bubble bottles were empty.

He was watching the clouds when he saw the strangest bubble.

It came nearer and nearer
and nearer until it landed.

Bibble climbed out of the spaceship.

Bobby **stared** at Bibble. Bibble **blinked** at Bobby.

"What's your name?" asked Bobby.

"Bibble" said Bibble.

"How did you get here?" asked Bobby.

"Bibblewibblebubble," said Bibble.

Bobby didn't understand.

So Bibble took some bubbles

and **twisted** and **pulled** to show him.

Then Bobby understood. So together,
they made some more bubble mixture.

with a **squeeze** of this, and a **drop** of that,

they had soon filled all the bottles.

When Bibble caught the
bubbles they didn't POP! Bibble could
make bubble animals, bubble buildings, even
bubble bicycles. Bicycles that he could ride!

Bobby wanted Bibble to stay forever.

But he saw the way that Bibble
watched the bubbles float away.

This world was not his home;
it was time to say goodbye.

Bobby watched as Bibble built his spaceship. Then he **waved** and **waved** until Bibble was just a bubble in the sky.

Bobby was not sure if blowing bubbles
would ever be the same again.

But then Bobby found a
special present waiting for him...

...A bubble that didn't POP!

And blowing bubbles is better than ever.

Now Bobby knows where the bubbles go...

...and Bibble knows where to find them.

The End

Bibble and the Bubbles
An original concept by author Alice Hemming
© Alice Hemming
Illustrated by Sara Sanchez

Published by MAVERICK ARTS PUBLISHING LTD
Studio 3A, City Business Centre, 6 Brighton Road,
Horsham, West Sussex, RH13 5BB
© Maverick Arts Publishing Limited, September 2014 +44 (0)1403 256941

A CIP catalogue record for this book is available at the British Library.

ISBN 978-1-84886-115-2

www.maverickbooks.co.uk